Angelina and Alice

Illustrations by Helen Craig   Story by Katharine Holabird

Clarkson N. Potter, Inc./Publishers NEW YORK
DISTRIBUTED BY CROWN PUBLISHERS, INC.

Angelina jumped for joy the day Alice came to school. Alice loved to dance and do gymnastics, and was good at all the same things as Angelina. They quickly became close friends and were always together. At breaks they skipped rope and did cartwheels round and round the playground.

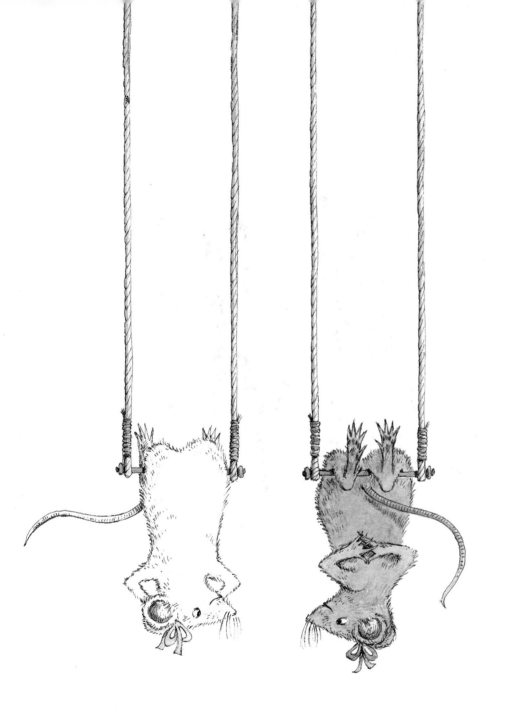

They loved to see who could
hang upside down longest
on the trapeze bar without
wiggling, swing highest on
the swings, or do the most
somersaults in the air.

Angelina was good at cartwheels and could even do the splits, but Alice could do a perfect handstand with her toes pointed straight in the air, and never lose her balance.

Angelina always fell over when she tried to do a handstand, which was embarrassing, especially on the playground.

One day Angelina fell right on her bottom and the older children pointed at her and laughed. One of them giggled and said, "Look at Angelina Tumbelina!" Another whispered to Alice, and then . . .

. . . something awful happened. Alice giggled too, and ran off to play with the older children while Angelina sat behind the swings and cried.

The next day was worse. They were all saying, "Angelina Tumbelina!" on the playground, and Angelina couldn't find Alice anywhere. Angelina couldn't concentrate at school and made lots of mistakes in her spelling. She couldn't eat her sandwiches at lunch either, and by the time the class was lining up for sports Angelina felt so sick she wished she could go home.

Mr Hopper, the sports teacher, blew his whistle for silence and said, "You've all worked so hard at your gymnastics over the year that we are going to do a show for the village festival. Everyone needs to find a partner and start practicing now."

Angelina looked at the floor. Who could she ask? She was afraid nobody would be her partner. A big tear rolled down her nose.

Then she felt a tap on her shoulder. It was Alice!
"Will you be my partner, please?" Alice asked.

All that afternoon Angelina and Alice
worked on handstands in the
gymnasium. "Just keep your head
down and line up your tail with the tip
of your nose," Alice said patiently.
"That always helps me to stay up
straight longer." Alice was a good
teacher, and soon Angelina could do
a handstand without falling at all.

Mr Hopper taught them
how to swing in a beautiful
circle over the bar, and how
to actually fly through the
air and land neatly balanced
on the mat.

He taught them to work with the rings and on the bars

and to do rhythmic gymnastics with colored ribbons.

Finally, Mr Hopper showed them a
terrific balancing trick they could do
for the show.

The day of the village festival was
bright and beautiful.

TODAY
A DISPLAY
OF
GYMNASTICS
BY THE
CHILDREN
OF
MOUSLE SCHOOL

The gymnastics class did a wonderful display at the village festival with high jumps, back flips and balancing on the bars. When Angelina and Alice did their balancing act together even the older children were impressed. "Wow!" they said, "how did you learn to do those amazing tricks?"

PIN THE TAIL ON THE CAT & WIN A PRIZE!

After the show, Mr Hopper smiled and
said, "That was really good teamwork!"
Alice and Angelina grinned back.
"That's because we're such good
friends," they said together.